What If Strawberries Had No Hats?

What If Strawberries Had No Hats?

A "Feel Better" Book for Children (and Adults) to Understand and Deal with Cancer

GRAPES

Written by Cassaundra Brown

Illustrations by June Gomez

RASPBERRIES

TOMATOES

CORN

BLUE-
BERRIES

STRAW-
BERRIES

A portion of the proceeds from the sale of this book is contributed to the University of California, Benioff Children's Hospital, San Francisco, Child Life Services (https://www.ucsfbenioffchildrens.org/services/child_life/)

Published by Byron Hot Springs
www.byronhotsprings.com

ISBN: 978-0-692-15095-5

Library of Congress Control Number: 2018954266

Origami instructions by: https://wikihow.com/Fold-Strawberry-Origami

Book design and composition by: Leigh McLellan Design

About the Type: Red titles and initial letters: Spumoni, designed by Garrett Boge in 1990, has bouncy, playful letters with a hand-drawn quality that infuse a sense of humor into headlines, titles and blurbs of text in need of a merry touch. *Text:* ITC Giovanni, designed in 1989, by California type designer Robert Slimbach. His goal was to create a face of classic old style proportions that is also thoroughly contemporary. The typeface has a modern feel with a larger x-height for accessibility and ease of reading.

FIRST EDITION

Printed in the United States of America in compliance with the Lacey Act by Ingram® Lightning Source®

Disclaimer: All errors and omissions are the responsibility of the author and illustrator.

Follow the adventures of Strawberry and all her Fruit Friends on Instagram and Facebook.

Dedicated to

Isiaha, Khamani, and Kelrhon

What if strawberries had no hats?
And they couldn't quite make it out of the patch.

And the berries so blue
Rolled out from their shrub

To embrace Strawberry
With a great big hug!

The kernels on the cob
Couldn't believe what they heard

And the grapes on the vine
Found it absurd.

So they paid Strawberry a visit
And much to their surprise,
She had lost her hat.
They couldn't believe their eyes!

"I have too many white seeds,
They outnumber the red.
And I have to stay strong,
'Tis what the doctor said."

"Ah ha!" Tomato said,
"Care and research will help you catch up.
You're not feeling your berry best.
We understand the fight is tough."

The cherries agreed
That this was the pits,

Then Apple fell from the tree
To tell Strawberry this...

19

"We will support you
And help you feel better,
With all of us here,
We are tougher than ...

20

Fruit leather!"

"What about my hat?"
Strawberry exclaimed!
Apple blushed with excitement,
"I'll try to explain,
If the Doc gives you treatment

In the patch where you stay,
She will take care of you.
You'll feel better this way."

Like Kiwi and Peach, you'll grow
A sprout or maybe fuzz.

Cousin Berry will razz everyone up,
The whole garden will be abuzz!

Strawberry chuckled,
"All I need is rest."

Lemon, Lime, and Orange added
"And perhaps a little zest!"

Banana will tell a few jokes,
Which are sure to have appeal.

Seeing you eye-to-eye,

Piña understands how you feel.

Onion will come to visit.
Out of happiness he'll cry,
"You have great friends who are here for you,
Sticking fruitfully by your side."

Our garden will flourish,

We'll be happy you're back.
You'll be the greatest hero
In the strawberry patch.

Our garden is filled with sunshine and love.
This is how we give back,
We take care of all strawberries,

Especially the Strawberries
Without any hats!

35

About the Author

Cassaundra Brown, a San Francisco, California, native, has always appreciated and participated in literary, musical, and culinary art expression. As an adolescent, Cassie's gift for writing was acknowledged by professors, fellow scholars, and peers. Her empathetic literary works afforded her opportunities to write short, informal essays, poems, and speeches for professional organizations. After graduating as a pastry chef in 2016, Cassaundra volunteered in charitable endeavors including the UCSF Benioff Children's Hospital Pediatric Oncology Clinic in San Francisco, California. It was not until a serendipitous acquisition of a strawberry plant that the inspiration for *What If Strawberries Had No Hats?* found verse. A portion of the proceeds from this book are contributed to children's cancer care. You can contact the author by email at whatifstrawberryhnh@gmail.com.

About the Illustrator

June Gomez resides in Brentwood, California, with her husband, three sons, one dog, and two geckos. Visual arts are her life passion. June's own artistic gifts were revealed to her in the third grade while creating her very first Christmas party placemat. In her youth, a sketchbook was her constant companion. Professional education and a bachelor of fine arts degree from the Academy of Art College, San Francisco, polished and expanded June's artistic abilities and technique. Her productive 30-year career includes commercial and residential mural painting, illustration, and custom fine art. June uses her artistic talent to enliven the visual art of storytelling herein with the creation of Strawberry and all the supportive Fruit Friends. You can learn more about the illustrator of *What If Strawberries Had No Hats?* at http://masterpiecemurals.net.

How to Fold a Strawberry Origami

With grateful thanks and to learn more and to view a video instructional guide,
please visit "Wiki How to Do Anything" at https://wikihow.com/Fold-Strawberry-Origami

1. Make sure that the sheet is double-sided—one green side and one red side. Check that you have the right origami paper.

2. Lay the green side up.

3. Fold one corner diagonally to the other. Crease the fold.

4. Take one corner on the creased side and fold it to the other corner on the same side. Crease the sides.

5. Lift one side of the triangle and open up the triangle so it creates a diamond-like shape. Crease the sides.

6. Turn over paper and repeat the previous step. Remember to crease the sides.

7. Turn the diamond-shaped origami paper around so that the opened folds are at the top and the closed corner is at the bottom.

8. Fold one side of the diamond into the middle. Do the same for the parallel side.

9. Unfold the kite-shaped origami paper. It should look like a diamond with the open ends at the top.

10. Put your index finger into the open end and slightly lift up one of the corners. Fold the side corner inward. Do the same for the parallel side.

11. Turn the folded origami over and repeat the process on this side as well.

12. Fold the side of the top of one corner of the kite-shaped origami towards the middle. Do the same for the parallel side, as well as the other two sides.

13. Lift the top of the kite-shaped origami and fold it downward. Crease the fold. Repeat for all sides.

14. Flip the origami to the sides that are fully red.

15. Fold the upper corner to the middle. Create a minor fold—not one that will extend to the side corner. Repeat for the other three sides.

16. Fold two sides together so that the minor folds are inside and the leaves are at each corner.

17. Blow into the hole that is at the top of the leaves.

18. Refer to the image to see the final product.

CPSIA information can be obtained at www.ICGtesting.com
Printed in the USA
BVIW120244070619
550165BV00001B/3